CHILDREN OF THE FORCE

Adapted by Kirsten Mayer

Grosset & Dunlap
An Imprint of Penguin Group (USA) Inc.
LucasBooks

GROSSET & DUNLAP

Published by the Penguin Group

Penguin Group (USA) Inc., 375 Hudson Street, New York, New York 10014, USA

Penguin Group (Canada), 90 Eglinton Avenue East, Suite 700, Toronto, Ontario M4P 2Y3, Canada

(a division of Pearson Penguin Canada Inc.)

Penguin Books Ltd., 80 Strand, London WC2R 0RL, England

Penguin Group Ireland, 25 St. Stephen's Green, Dublin 2, Ireland

(a division of Penguin Books Ltd.)

Penguin Group (Australia), 250 Camberwell Road, Camberwell, Victoria 3124, Australia

(a division of Pearson Australia Group Pty. Ltd.)

Penguin Books India Pvt. Ltd., 11 Community Centre, Panchsheel Park, New Delhi—110 017, India

Penguin Group (NZ), 67 Apollo Drive, Rosedale, North Shore 0632, New Zealand

(a division of Pearson New Zealand Ltd.)

Penguin Books (South Africa) (Pty.) Ltd., 24 Sturdee Avenue,

Rosebank, Johannesburg 2196, South Africa

Penguin Books Ltd., Registered Offices:

80 Strand, London WC2R 0RL, England

Library of Congress Cataloging-in-Publication Data is available.

ISBN 978-0-448-45338-5   10 9 8 7 6 5 4 3 2 1

The galaxy is at war! The Jedi generals and their trusty clone troopers fight for the Republic, protecting planets from Separatist invaders.
The evil Darth Sidious has hired a bounty hunter named Cad Bane to steal a Holocron—which contains a list of all the children in the galaxy who could one day grow up to be Jedi.

The Jedi Council knew that they must stop Bane.
"There are thousands of children on that list," said Master
Obi-Wan Kenobi. "Which will he go after first?"
"Through the Force," replied Jedi Master Yoda, "the
Council may detect them."

The Jedi Masters invited Jedi Knight Anakin Skywalker to sit with them as they tried to locate disturbances in the Force.

"A jungle world with domed cities, I see," said Yoda. "Rodia, it is."

"I see it, too," said Obi-Wan.

"I sense a place I've been to before . . . Naboo," said Anakin.
Yoda looked up at Anakin. "To Naboo you must go."
Obi-Wan stood up and declared that he would go to Rodia.
The two Jedi left to try and get to the children before
Bane did.

On the planet Rodia, a mother proudly watched her little boy named Wee Duun use the Force to lift his ball off the ground. A man dressed as a Jedi was watching the boy, too. "He will make a fine Jedi," the man said. "For your son's protection, I'm going to have to take him now."

The mother was not going to let the man take her son, so he used a device called a hypnogazer to put her into a trance. This was no Jedi—it was Cad Bane in disguise! He grabbed Wee Duun and ran off.

Obi-Wan arrived moments later. With a wave of his hand, Obi-Wan used the Force to snap the mother out of the trance.

"Where is the bounty hunter?" asked Obi-Wan.

"Bounty hunter?" The mother blinked. "Oh no!"

The Jedi ran to an open window, just in time to see Bane carry the child onto his starship and blast off!

Bane's next stop was the planet Naboo. The bounty hunter snuck into a child's bedroom and went over to a crib. When he yanked back the blanket, Bane got a big surprise—the baby wasn't there!

Ahsoka Tano appeared behind the villain with her lightsaber ready. "Don't move, sleemo!" she yelled.

Bane quickly knocked the lightsaber from Ahsoka's hands. He used his hover boots to fly up through the ceiling of the house. But there was another surprise waiting—Anakin Skywalker!

The Jedi and his Padawan quickly captured Bane and took him aboard their starship. The Naboo child was safe.

But Bane had already sent two children to Darth Sidious. Nanny droids cared for the babies as a hologram of Darth Sidious appeared in the nursery. The babies began to cry. One of the nanny droids spoke to the hologram. "Sir, I think they may be too young for the training."

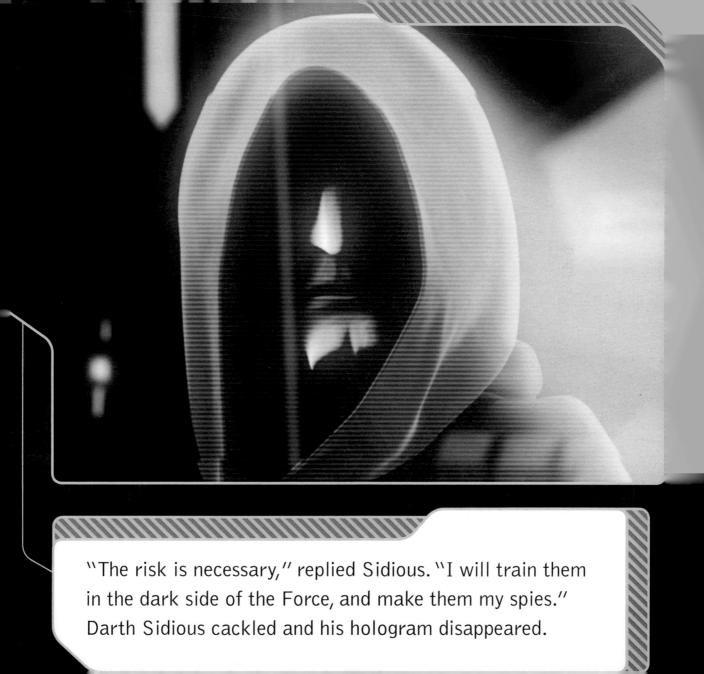

"The risk is necessary," replied Sidious. "I will train them in the dark side of the Force, and make them my spies." Darth Sidious cackled and his hologram disappeared.

Back on the Jedi cruiser, the Jedi questioned the bounty hunter, but he would not speak. So they used the Force to try to get the truth from him.

"You *will* take us to the Holocron," Anakin ordered the villain.

"Your Jedi mind tricks don't work on me," said Bane. After a while, however, Bane was tired from trying to keep the Jedi out of his mind. He finally said he would take them to the Holocron and the kidnapped children.

Obi-Wan and Mace Windu loaded Bane onto their shuttle.
"This could be a trap," Anakin said. "Are you sure you
don't need us to go?"
Mace Windu replied, "Of course it's a trap, Skywalker."
"I will contact you when we find the Holocron and the
children," Obi-Wan said.

The shuttle lifted off and set out into space.

"What if they don't find those kids?" Ahsoka asked.

"They will," Anakin said. "Come on, we need to look at Bane's ship more closely."

Anakin sat in the cockpit of Bane's ship as Ahsoka inspected the landing gear. She scraped off some black ash and looked at it.

"Hmmm, Bane picked up a lot of volcanic ash in his travels," she said.

"If we cross-reference the planets we know he visited with the amount of fuel he used . . ." Anakin said.

"We can calculate where else he went!" exclaimed Ahsoka. Anakin scrolled through the names of the planets until he came to Mustafar.

"Wait," said Ahsoka. "That would explain the ash on his landing gear. I think it's worth looking into."

"Let's go!" said Anakin.

Meanwhile, Bane led Obi-Wan and Mace Windu to a remote system. They landed the shuttle on Black Stall Station, where Bane had his secret headquarters.
"I don't sense any children nearby," said Obi-Wan.

They entered an elevator that took them up several levels
into a large, open room. They could see the Holocron
glowing blue across the dark room.

"Let me get it for you," offered Bane.

"You've done enough," said Mace Windu.

As soon as Windu went to get the Holocron, an alarm went off. Lights flashed and electricity surged through the floor. He leaped into the air and jumped onto a box of crates. Bane smiled and jumped to a ledge on the wall. "So long, Jedi!" he called.

Laser beams began to shoot in all directions and the two Jedi Masters deflected the blasts with their lightsabers. Obi-Wan somersaulted across the room to reach the Holocron. He grabbed it and the two Jedi made their way back to the elevator platform.

Anakin and Ahsoka landed on Mustafar. A lake of fiery lava surrounded the landing platform and a small building. "You sure this is the right place?" asked Ahsoka. "We're gonna find out," said Anakin.

They entered a dark, spooky hallway.

"I sense something, Master," said the Padawan with a shiver. "I don't like it."

"It's the dark side, Ahsoka. We're in the right place."

Suddenly, they heard a baby cry.

Inside the building's nursery, the nanny droids were still watching over the two children. An alarm alerted them that a ship had landed outside. The hologram of Darth Sidious reappeared. "Evacuate the children to my other facility!"

"We must destroy all the evidence! Turn off the gravity
supports and let the building sink into the lava," Darth
Sidious ordered.
One of the nanny droids punched a series of buttons
and the room lurched and tilted to one side. Each droid
grabbed a crying child and turned to leave.

Anakin and Ahsoka slowly entered the dark room.
"The babies are gone!" Ahsoka cried as she saw the empty cribs.
"I can sense they're still here," said Anakin as the two nanny droids came out of the shadows.

The two Jedi fought the nanny droids, while watching out for the babies. Ahsoka slashed at the droid's weapons, but the floor beneath her gave way and hot lava shot up through the opening. She leaped up the wall to safety.

Ahsoka reached out and grabbed the baby just before the
nanny droid fell into the pit.
Across the room, Anakin used the Force to pull the other
baby into his arms before defeating the second nanny droid.

They got back onto their ship just in time to see the building pulled under the surface of the lava. Ahsoka cradled both children, while Anakin piloted the ship home. Both kids were safe!

Back on Coruscant, Anakin and Ahsoka met with the Jedi Council.

"The children are safe, and back home again," said Obi-Wan with a smile.

Once again, the future of the Jedi was safe . . . at least for now.